Effie
Enjoy reading!
Charlotte Levenson

Ricki
the Warlock

Charlotte Levenson

Published by Charlotte Levenson

Copyright © Charlotte Levenson 2014

For Ricki (not the warlock!)
Without you the words would not of made it
this far. You manage to without fail make
me laugh every day. Keep up the good work,
it's not as messy as tears and cheaper than
medicine!

To Mum and Oliver for your love and
support, and to Dad who laughs with us
from above.

Ricki
the Warlock

Ricki
the Warlock

Chapter 1

Getting to know me

If you look up the meaning of 'Warlock' on Wikipedia then you will read the following -

"A magician is someone who uses or practices magic that derives from supernatural or occult sources."

That is what I am. A Warlock, and my name is Ricki. I am twelve years and four months old. Now I know what you are thinking already; that a Warlock is a character made in fantasy and fiction but I can assure you that we really are real. Obviously for good reason the powers above allow me to look like a 'normal' twelve year old should do, as to not draw too much attention to myself in my everyday life, but apart from my youthful (good) looks I am actually very different from everyone else and I wouldn't change a thing.

I wasn't born from Warlock blood – neither my mother nor father has any supernatural power, in fact they are pretty run of the mill (I mean that in the nicest possible way). My dad (Edward or Ed as he's known to most) is an electrician, he has his own business so he works for himself with his mate Dave as his wingman; and my mum (Karen) works down the local retirement home as a hairdresser for the old folks. Dad 'occasionally' says that mum is a witch when she is out of the room but I doubt very much he means that literally as he has no idea what a real witch is like – I obviously do because I have crossed paths with many in my time as a Warlock but I don't divulge such information to Dad and just tend to agree with him as far as mum goes.

I live in a small town just outside London called Bandel and unfortunately I would like to tell you that I reside in a Castle with a cone shaped tower but instead my

3

headquarters are a very modest three bedroomed semi; and although it doesn't have huge wrought iron gates and a long driveway leading up to it, it has however got a humongous old tree in the back garden that Dad said is hundreds of years old; and it is in this great tree that Dad himself built me a tree house; or as I refer to it Warlock HQ. It's a marvellous place and it is in this very tree house that I was picked by the Magician Lords to become a Warlock back when I was eight years and seven months.

Now the Magician Lords don't ever visit you in person, that's not how it works; it's not like their just a bunch of old guys in cloaks sat around on a couch somewhere, with a cuppa and a biscuit waiting for the next Warlock to appear – these guys are busy, double busy you could even say – they haven't got time to travel all over the place

having face to face meetings with future young Warlocks, it would take too long – everyone would start asking them a million questions and wanting to chit chat as people do and before you know it, BAM a quick five minute trip to do a Warlock initiation has turned into dinner with the family and a selfie at the end for keep sakes.

So for this reason they keep it short and sweet – all that happens is they send you a sign like a shooting star or a bolt of lightning strikes and you feel something change, right through to your finger tips, like you have suddenly been given a secret power – and of course you have that's the whole point.

I know what you're probably thinking 'Yeah right Ricki, whatever' but I swear it's true my information is gold, it came from a reputable source, a former Warlock actually – Geoffrey was his name – proper guy he was, an old fashioned gentleman as mum says. I first met him at the retirement home where my mum works as it happens, I can't remember exactly why now but for some reason I had to go into work with mum that day – a Saturday it was and I can just remember being rather unhappy about the whole thing at the time because as we all know Saturdays are a school free day and I had planned to spend mine in the good company of my PS4 but mum had other plans; so as always she ruined mine, and I ended up at the retirement home without much say in the matter.

I was sat quietly (sulking) in the lounge with the old folks, spacing out to some morning talk show on the TV when a really tall man walked in. He had a massive white beard but his hair was still like a dark grey colour – looked weird I'm not going to lie to you – anyway this odd looking fella came and sat next to me – 'GREAT' I thought, out of all the seats in this room the retired Santa Claus has to park up by me – just my luck. Anyway after a quick introduction and a bit of polite nattering, Geoffrey comes out with this little corker,

"Ricki – you are born to be a Warlock and your initiation will soon be upon you – it is a special gift, use it wisely."

I cracked up – this guy is off his rocker – "Alright Geoffrey you little joker, where did that come from? Didn't have you down as a funny man," I said to him.

He went on to tell me that I had always known that I was different from the other kids – and to be frank Geoffrey's got a point, I did notice a few inconsistencies in the similarities shared amongst all the other kids and myself and come to think of it, I was always the one at birthday parties I was invited to that worked out how the clowns did their tricks – used to drive the poor fellas mad – there they were just trying to earn a decent living, put food on the table and a roof over the heads of the wife and kids, dressed up as a clown entertaining the likes of us at parties with a few card tricks and some animal shaped balloons; and then there was me, front row, shouting out how

they were doing it and spoiling the act –
must of hated me. Although it wasn't done
with any malice I can assure you – I'm not
that sort of boy I just knew the answers
that's all.

Geoffrey told me a few ins and outs of the
Warlock trade that Saturday morning
including how the initiation process works
with the Magician Lords – which he has
never met either as it happens, but I will be
eternally grateful for the knowledge and
wisdom hc shared with me that day. He
passed away shortly after we met – god rest
his soul – gutted I was to be honest – reckon
I could of learnt a lot off that old boy and
had some right laughs along the way.
Dynamite he was. RIP old man.

Anyways I, Ricki of Bandel was one night
chosen by the Magician Lords when a bolt of
lightning hit my tree house and from then on

I was the only one allowed in Warlock HQ –
discretion is the key with magic and I etched
in the front door the Magic Circle motto
'Indocilis Privata Loqui' which means 'not
apt to disclose secrets', but I just told mum
and dad it meant 'Private Keep Out' in
Spanish to avoid questions – like I said
discretion is the key.

Chapter 2

The outfit

I know you're probably wondering what us Warlocks wear on a day to day basis – well Monday to Friday 9am – 3.30pm I wear like all the other children a school uniform – a restrictive shirt and tie with a heavy wool jumper and a tailored trouser – all in grey apart from the tie, that is red; but on evenings, weekends, school holidays, bank holidays and teacher training days I wear my distinctive pointed hat and Warlock cloak. The cloak was crafted by the hands of a generation past. A group of women that have their hair done by my mum as it happens, and they belong to a club that goes by the name of 'The Knitting Circle'.

When mum told me such women were kindly going to make me a cloak I was shocked that it did not come with some terms and conditions, as normally these women are bound by a supernatural force and not always a good one – I thought at the time that if they somehow knew of the power I had been given that maybe they would weave evil through the fabric in a bid to restrain my power; but as it happens it fits just perfect – and a great length that gives just the right amount of swing as I walk to create dramatic effect when I need it; and it's actually very light and airy – I often wonder why they haven't caught on in the High Street stores.

The cloak itself is black with a border of silver and gold stars and half moons sewn onto the bottom and around the edges of the sleeves and my pointed hat is all black with my name on the inside. I don't have a wand or a cauldron because they are for witches and that Potter kid and I don't want to get involved in spells and quidditch; I just need to hone my craft quietly behind the scenes in

Warlock HQ until I can one day reveal my
true self to all as 'Ricki The Great Warlock';

but until then I have to practice, practice, practice because creating magic doesn't come easy and I am still in my apprentice stages.

Oh, and by the way just in case you were wondering after my initiation at Warlock HQ ... I don't have a long white beard. Couple of reasons for this,

I can't physically grow a beard yet especially a long white one.

And

That would just be weird – a twelve-year-old kid with a full Warlock beard – not even I could pull that one off.

Just thought 'I would straighten that out as I don't want any confusion as to what I look like – beards arc commonly associated with Warlocks and no doubt one day I will indeed have the full long white beard but I'm just not quite ready yet. Got to get hairy armpits first!

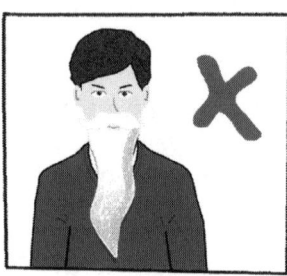

Chapter 3

My W.A.

My best friend Gary Watts is a really nice guy. So much so that back when I was ten and three months I made Gary my official WA (Warlock assistant). With great power comes great responsibility I explained to Gary and for that reason I was going to have my hands full so having him around would lighten the load. Although first he had to take an oath (written by me);

"Do you Gary Watts swear to the magical lords above and to I Ricki the Warlock of Bandel – current status apprentice, that you will remain silent and not share any information you hear or supernatural that you see to any other source such as television, newspapers and any members of the general public that includes family and pets."

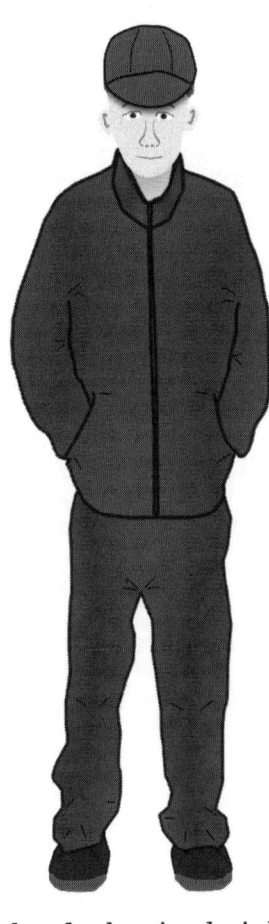

Mum said Gary is from a 'salt of the earth' family, which basically means their good-hearted folk. Gary's a lot shorter than me in height but to be honest he never had much chance of getting back row of the school photograph coming from his mum and dad, they're both short as well, in fact the whole Watts family are under 5ft 5ins; but what he lacks in height he makes up for in humour – funniest guy I know, and if you ever have a 'Pick n mix' dilemma then Gary's your man. The knowledge this fella is packing when it comes to sweets is breathtaking; don't think there's a sweet he hasn't tried yet. I must say I've learnt a lot from Gary in this department and now I have a much softer pallet when it comes to choosing my 'Pick n Mix' – it's all about the quality now not quantity and Gary knows all the reputable sources to get just the right gear from. So if you're looking for a top of the range sweet bag with the finest white mice, fruit salad, bumper bananas and double dips then look no further – Gary's your man. What this fella doesn't know about sweets just isn't worth knowing.

We are in the same form class at school and he lives across the road from my house – Gary's job most evenings is to sit outside Warlock HQ and keep guard whilst I brush up on new powers. Then when I have them mastered I reveal each one to him and he

claps and tells me how amazing it is –
although we have had a few disasters – like
the time I tried to cut down a branch from
the tree just using my mind, but didn't
realize that there was a strong magnetic
force in Bandel that evening, and as the
power ran through my body and out my
finger tips towards the carefully selected
branch (Gary's job), the force hit the
magnetic field and bounced back chopping
the peak off Gary's cap!! We put it down to a
rookie error and I promised Gary I would
learn how to attach things as well as detach
in the future and fix his hat, but for now he
just wears it without a peak which is a
unique look I'm not going to lie, and that's
saying something coming from the boy in a
cloak and pointed hat!

I have come a long way since then and can
do most of what I refer to as 'the basics'

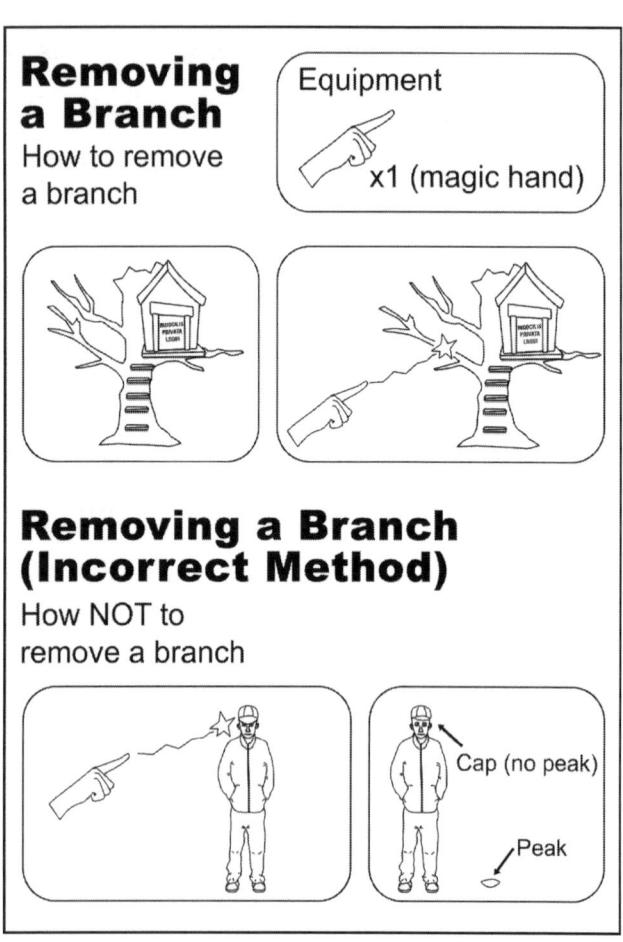

without much thought anymore and these have come in very handy at times during school hours for Gary and I. I know your probably thinking that both me and Gary are the most popular kids in school because I am a Warlock and Gary my WA but unbelievably this is not the case, and we like I am sure many of you out there, have had our fair share of meetings with bullies and still do occasionally to this day although they are a little wary of me now all because of an incident that happened one year ago when I was eleven and four months. I'll tell you all about it.

Chapter 4

Easter Weekend

It all started on Easter weekend. Every year at this time the retirement home that mum works at has children in from the area to perform different talents in front of the residents. You have the usual singing (sometimes not in tune) and dancing (sometimes involves twerking which is highly inappropriate for the occasion) from local dance groups or daughters and sons of employees wanting to perform with their bands or boy/girl groups; but this year Gary and I had decided to put on a magic show. After much deliberation at Warlock HQ we decided that it would be a good idea for me to practice some of the more popular magic tricks for example pick a card, shuffle cup and the timeless hanky from my sleeve.

The show was just to get me used to using my power in more public situations as opposed to just at Warlock HQ; and not

because I wanted to be the next Paul Daniels
(cringe), but as Gary quite rightly pointed
out to me, I might need to save a life or
create a diversion to avoid accident for the
greater good at some point in the future, and
I can't be feeling any extra pressure from
random people watching me – the magic had
to flow in any situation. He was absolutely
right, and it's advice like this at times like

these that remind me exactly why I gave Gary this very important job as my WA.

So we practiced every night for two weeks until we had (in our opinions) a flawless routine that would without doubt get some old people out of their seats clapping – well not literally because half of them can't get up without a hoist, but you get the idea.

My grandma and granddad came over the house on Good Friday as they do every year. They only live twenty minutes away and normally come to our house for Sunday lunch every other week religiously but on Easter Weekend they visit on the Friday. Old people love routine, that's what mum says anyway and she would know she sees enough of them. Grandma is my dad's mum and she always makes such a fuss of him when she first arrives; it's a bit sickly really he looks about ten years old when she does it; and I know mum doesn't like it because she always just says hello to grandpa and then walks off into the kitchen, muttering under her breath, something about old and cow but we hardly ever have roast beef so I never understand what she means.

Granddad on the other hand is pretty cool for an old guy, he always tells me the best stories about when he was growing up; Tales of magic and mystery and people that he's met over the years. Granddad isn't a Warlock in case you were wondering – well I'm 99.9% sure he isn't anyway. I don't know if the stories he tells me have any truth in them or if they are all made up on the spot but either way they are always good to hear and that's all that matters really. Nan gets cross with granddad for telling me these stories – says it gives me an overactive imagination and that's not good for me but granddad just rolls his eyes, nods and says *"Right you are sweetheart, no more stories."* But before I can even pull a sad face he's turned his head given me a cheeky little wink and told me the key to living in peace (his opinion)… "Just tell them what they want to hear son". Sound advice, especially where Nan's concerned because once she starts nagging she's like a dog with a bone. There's no one in our family that can get me to tidy my room quicker than Nan. Just the thought of her nagging makes me bolt up the stairs and start putting things away. I'm not pulling your chain here I promise that woman's nagging can literally wear you down until you are exhausted just listening to her voice – it's like a super power that drains you into submission.

Apart from that she's a proper bird my Nan and blinding in the kitchen – which I'm guessing is why granddad loves her so much. I've never come across another guy that loves cakes as much as granddad. He can put the biggest of slices away and still come back for more – a legend in his own right and a skill I hope he has passed down to me – I just pray I get to keep my own set of teeth though!

I don't know if you've ever seen a set of false teeth floating in a glass at the side of the bed before but be warned it's a shock to the system; took the wind right out of my sails when I first came face to face with the gnashers. I've only seen granddads though, not Nan's; reckon if they caught site of me they would start nagging – even in a glass!

Anyhow, I told granddad all about the magic show me and Gary were doing on Sunday at the retirement home and he thought it was a great idea, he was so enthusiastic about my pending debut that I told him I would give everyone a sneak preview in the lounge. Parents and grandparents at the ready I started to perform my magic show even though I was minus Gary so they didn't get the full effect but at least got the gist of it. Hanky out of the sleeve was awesome, shuffle cup had them all laughing but my card trick blew their minds - especially when I pulled the mystery Jack of Diamonds from Nan's handbag. I finished with a round of applause from everyone and took a well-deserved bow. Mum was like 'That's brilliant Ricki how do you do that?' Obviously I'm never going to tell her that would break the code of magic so I just tap my index finger against the end of my nose and say, "Now that would be telling."

Grandma loves to harper on about dad

and how proud she is of him having his own business – at any given opportunity she will pipe up and start preaching to me about how I should look up to my father for all he's achieved and sooner or later I would have to take off my "silly cloak and hat" and start to knuckle down at school if I am going to one day take over the family business BLAH, BLAH, BLAH!

"You're not serious about this magic idea are you Ricki? I mean what do you want to do when you leave school?" said grandma

"I want to be a Warlock." I answer and as I look over to mum she is trying to hold back the laughter because she thinks I have just said this to wind Nan up, but in fact I am serious even though no one in the room thinks I am.

Nan starts to moan at mum and dad about how they shouldn't laugh at me or encourage such ridiculous answers but granddad just adds fuel to the fire by shouting out *"well being a Warlock sounds pretty damn good to me what's the salary like these days?"*, Everyone laughed especially when I told them that you don't get money just an unlimited supply of white birds and hankies.

They laughed. But what's funny about that I thought!

Chapter 5

The old folks home

Easter Sunday arrived and Gary and I were as prepared as we could possibly be for the show – we had decided that Gary should wear something a bit smarter for the show but his wardrobe is limited to his school uniform or jogging bottoms and t-shirts in an assortment of colours; so smarter joggers and a smarter t-shirt is what we settled for – all in black because we've heard both our mums say when they get ready to go out that they can't go wrong with black, and this is important because we really don't want anything to go wrong in the show. It's funny what advice you pick up from your parents without them realizing.

We arrived at the retirement home and waited in the hall with our box of tricks until it was our turn – the act before was thankfully a flop – a nice looking girl but she murdered the high bit in the song and old people are cut throat, they didn't even clap at the end. Any way her loss was our gain, and Gary and I sailed through the show – mum was watching the whole time along with some of her work colleagues and their children; there was one kid though at the back of the room that had a right miserable face and didn't laugh once – obviously not a magic fan. Gary did decide to wear his peak-less cap which I wasn't over keen on as it made the 'smart' tracksuit look a little less so but the main thing is we got through it and it went down a treat with the audience. Everyone was laughing and clapping and I finished this time by pulling the chosen card from behind an old man's ear – Harold was his name and he had humongous ears but was slightly deaf – funny that – any way they were the perfect size to pull a card from.

The clapping went on a little longer than we expected and Gary and I ended up bowing like four times before leaving the stage - we felt like rock stars.

I like it at the retirement home, it's not too sloppy there. The nurses seem to run a tight ship but manage to keep a friendly

'nursing home ambience' at the same time –
not an easy task in my opinion. Mums boss,
Maureen, is always organizing things for the
old folks to keep them entertained. I like this
about her – makes getting old not seem so
bad; but when I'm that age Maureen will be
six foot under – bless her soul – so I'm just
hoping her enthusiasm for the job keeps
getting past down a generation, otherwise
we're screwed! Well I'm not because I'm a
Warlock and can do spells but poor Gary he
could be sat in the same chair for days!

Anyway like I was saying it's pretty good
at this retirement home – I mean I'd love to
just get up on a morning have some
breakfast, someone wash and dress me but
let me keep my slippers on – mooch on into
the lounge, pick a seat and have people come
and put on a show for me. Not half bad if you
ask me. I guess being old is kinda like being

a kid – people doing stuff for you – picking your clothes and meals and organizing things to keep you quiet – funny that, when you're a kid you can't wait to be a grown up and when you are a grown up you get treated like a kid! Makes no sense really.

That night, after the show Gary and I sat in Warlock HQ and talked over and over again about our performance and what a rush it gave us. Gary suggested mid conversation that we enter for our annual school talent show. I wasn't sure taking the show big time was the right move to make but like Gary said I have been given an amazing gift and why shouldn't I bring some enjoyment to peoples' lives with it – and he was right again – just look at the old folks earlier on for example, they lapped it up. Sink or swim I thought to myself, let's do it!

We decided our stage name would be

'Magicki' a mixture of Ricki and magic and we would perform the same tricks as we did at the retirement home but maybe slightly extended versions. We were both excited; this show was going to make us popular and cool at school without doubt.

Chapter 6

The bullies

I met Gary as I usually do every day outside his house so we can walk to school together. It was the Tuesday after Easter Monday and so we had a short week at school. HAPPY DAYS! Gary and I set off on our usual route to school, which involves a pit stop at the off license to buy sweets with a small percentage of our dinner money. The 'offy' as we call it is owned and run by a Turkish guy called Ali – really nice fella but part wolf I think – he's short, fat and the hairiest bloke I have ever seen; I'm talking arms, legs and even his back (I can see it crawling up his neck out of his t-shirt) and it's thick black like the hair on his head.

I can't imagine ever being that hairy – suppose it keeps you warm in the winter but the heat in the summer would really do you in. Saying that there's a handful of boys in my year at school that have random facial

hair and have grown a foot taller than everyone else – you must have seen them, I think they are in every school and the teachers always stand them on the back row of the school photo. You would rather be on their side when we are made to play rugby in PE, but you do NOT want to get down wind of these guys when they get hot – Jesus the smell they let off makes your toes curl! I was telling mum and dad about it over dinner one night – mum said it's normal and all part of growing up and becoming a man – she said that their parents should buy them a deodorant spray that stops the smell – or as dad mildly puts it *"no there's no excuse for being stinky – they need introducing to the can!"*

Anyways don't be put off by Ali the hairy shopkeeper because the guy knows his sweets and always stocks the best gear; and he keeps the place tidy and organized as well so I know where things are – I like that and I'll tell you something else for nothing as well in all my time as a customer I've never noticed a random hair from his wolf like coat anywhere on site; No stray hairs ending up in your sweet mix at this shop – Ali's fur is tight to the root – no shedding which is impressive in my opinion!

The only slightly odd thing is that he calls everyone 'Brother'.

"Alright Ricki brother" he goes but I just roll with it and say "Alright bruv" and get my sweets – I can't tell you why he does this because there's no chance in hell we are brothers – I've not even been to Turkey on holiday!

On this particular day when we came out of Ali's shop a group of boys from our school were outside. They were the school bullies. I had seen them around and in some of my classes but thankfully had never come into direct contact with them.

Their gang consisted of a boy called

Damien or 'Dunce' which is his nickname. He is the main boy and calls all the shots – he is very tall for his age and although his height is intimidating his brain power definitely is not, as he always uses words in sentences that don't make sense to anyone but him and this makes him a little amusing – although obviously I never laugh directly at him or in any eye shot what so ever just in case!

The other boy is Martin aka Chunk, he's the weight behind the gang, literally, the boy has three chins and is never seen not eating – his pockets are always crammed with food. He is huge compared to Gary and me, I think his head alone weighs more than the two of us put together; and finally there is Seth aka Death Breath Seth. He is tall and skinny and just repeats everything Dunce says like a parrot, or randomly shouts out

'Yeah' in agreement with something Dunce has said. It's very bizarre to see.

Gary has some classes with Death Breath Seth and he said that we should not take his nickname lightly he genuinely has the most rotten breath in the world! Gary said it's like a super power that could melt your face if over exposed to its chemicals, and that on more than one occasion he has been tempted to launch a mint into his mouth from afar when Seth has yawned, just to try and take the edge off the smell, but he has not yet had the courage to actually throw the polo.

Anyway as we left the off license with our sweets Dunce jumped into our path saying -

"Well look who we have here, it's magic trick boy. Why don't you show us a trick, what's the matter got nothing up your arm?"

I silently presumed he meant sleeve not arm but thought it best not to correct him, no one likes a smart ass, that's what mum says to dad. Gary and I kept our heads down and carried on walking around the gang but as we did they were shouting at us -

"You will do a trick for us you hear!"

And Gary out of nowhere shouts "Yeah we will at the talent show and you can give us a clap for it too!"

Now I don't know what Gary was thinking shouting back especially when I've got my hands full of my favourite sweets – but it prompted the gang to start to chase us – NOT GOOD!!

We made it to the school gates – our sweets intact thank God, but only just and Dunce shouted-

"You won't get away with that again, you two better watch your backs".

We had a lucky escape this time but Gary wasn't too bothered because he just said that if push comes to shove then I will have to use some magic to restrain them from getting us but I wasn't so keen on this idea – I don't think starting a war is the right way to go, but that doesn't mean to say that if a random dog poo happened to move from the grass to the pavement that the bullies walk home on that I wouldn't have some explaining to do! I mean no one likes to stand in dog poop even bullies. We might have to watch our backs but those three fools need to watch their feet!

I mentioned to my mum about Damien and his friends but she said that he was probably just jealous because of the magic show we put on at the retirement home. You see I didn't realize at the time but the miserable boy I noticed at the back of the room that day when we did our show was in fact Damien (Dunce). His mum works with my mum at the retirement home and Damien had to go to work with his mum that Easter Sunday because his dad was out watching the footie. That explains why he suddenly just appeared on the Tuesday shouting things about magic to us. Mum was definitely right it must come from jealously and frankly I don't blame him, the magic show really was good, I know I mentioned it earlier but the applause did go on long enough for us to bow four times. Dunce was clearly unhappy at our success and wants to try and ruin it. Sad really. I can't help that I'm a Warlock; it's just my trade.

The rest of the week had both horrific and hilarious moments at school for Gary and I. The bullies continued to taunt us on the way to school, during breaks and on the way home (that's the horrific bit) but for some reason Dunce never quite followed through with all the nasty threats he spoke; I mean that's a good thing because some of them were terribly unpleasant.

I think he must secretly be wary of myself and Gary, he can't quite work us out – the fear of the unknown, obviously if he wanted to start on us you think he would of done it by now – he was definitely up to something. Guess we will just have to wait it out and hope we can deal with whatever he and his bully sidekicks throw at us.

Chapter 7

Drawn order

Rehearsals for the school talent show were taking place everywhere around school. Gymnastics, dance, drama, music – you name it our school had it. We, on the other hand were keeping rehearsals strictly to Warlock HQ; due to the nature of our act it had to be kept secret until the day for the full effect. We were quietly confident however that we looked slightly better than what we could see around school.

Dunce and his gang had kept their distance over the last few days – I was praying that they had grown tired of us and had maybe moved on – but every now and then our paths would cross in a corridor and he and his merry men would glare at us with hatred in their eyes – well Dunce and Seth did but Chunk looked more hungry than anything else – how this is possible I don't know because he was eating a foot long baguette at the time. Still it made me feel a little uneasy both the staring and the amount of mayonnaise in his baguette!

With just two days to go the order list of acts for the show was placed on the notice board in reception at school. Everyone gathered to see if they had been drawn first – no one wanted that position; the audience is cold and hungry for entertainment. Thankfully a girl named Helen Davies got it and she was singing solo – from what I can recall from music lessons Helen had quite a good voice so she should be safe up there – I know the saying 'you'll get eaten alive' springs to mind but fortunately for Helen she's slim so maybe the crowd will be kind as there wouldn't be much to go around, you know if they ate her alive. Act two on the other hand –a boy band called 'Boytown' (cringe) well they were four well-fed boys! So pray for them because there's enough on those lads for a main and dessert!

Out of fifteen acts we were drawn last – there it was in black and white "Magicki". I had butterflies in my stomach – I would rather of gone somewhere in the middle – but Gary said that it's the perfect spot, save the best until last he said to me. I just hoped I didn't let him down – he was so excited. I was going to practice overtime for the next two days and make sure the act was clockwork.

Gary had to go around his Nan's that night – she has gout so she can't make it to their house – Gary said that one day her leg will fall off because of the gout but that won't mean she dies; just that his family will have a small funeral for the leg – which I will be invited too because he said his mum will more than likely bury it next to Wiggles the old pet budgie out back of the house. Any way with Gary at his Nan's it would give me chance to really focus on the tricks and maybe dust off a few more difficult ones that I had attempted in the past but hadn't had time to perfect – just in case.

I often wonder to myself if Gary will be part of my magic forever. I hope we stay friends – can't imagine life without him to be honest – I mean he drives me mad at times but he's always there, like a loyal dog and that's not easy to find these days in a person. I see other kids in school flitter between groups of friends every other week – I couldn't keep up; but Gary and I we just stick together and it seems to work.

I'd like to think that Gary will be my WA for good but you never know, when we leave school will be the decider I suppose. He might want to be a plumber or something along those lines – he always says that jobs like that are good to have, because when you fix things for people in their houses the mums always give you tea and biscuits whilst you work. Little things like that are important to Gary – that's why every now and then I use my powers to make his sweets twice the size – he loves it and it keeps him busy for hours – easily pleased I guess.

I could use my magic to give him whatever sweets his heart desired but I think I'd be making a rod for my own back with that one as Gary can seriously put it away and before you know it I'd be laying on a full spread everyday! I'd be more like a caterer than a Warlock!

Chapter 8

Last minute nerves

The day had dawned and with it brought the 'ANNUAL TALENT SHOW'. I didn't sleep a wink last night worrying over today's events and to be honest just all that could go wrong – which made me wonder if I was really cut out to be a Warlock as surely I should be fearless with nerves of steel, instead I am sleep deprived and riddled with worry.

Mum said that nerves are a good thing – try telling my legs that I thought – they have had to carry me up and down the stairs umpteen times this morning to use the bathroom (a dreadful side effect to nerves) but we shall say no more on that subject.

Gary on the other hand, cool as a cucumber. He saunters in my house all dressed in his 'smart trackie' with not a care in the world; I contemplated briefly getting cross with him for having such a nonchalant attitude towards our pending task but I stopped myself, after all I was clearly the one with issues here not Gary and having his calming approach towards the show around me was just what I needed.

"Cheer up Ricki stop thinking of all that could go wrong. Focus on our routine, enjoy yourself and chill out – you are an amazing Warlock with the best assistant in town – don't worry about mishaps that's my job, and I'm not worried because, we, Magicki, are brilliant!"

Gary is some assistant it has to be said – wise words from someone in a tracksuit and a peak-less cap and all before 8.30am but it was just what was needed to kick me into shape for the show.

School was buzzing, there was an air of tension and excitement that was filling the halls and rooms everywhere. Acts all over were cramming in the last few practices before the show started. Gary and I had decided not to join in with the last minute rehearsals but instead just dropped our box of props off with the stage team, and sat and ate our sweets we had bought on the way in. Ali the shopkeeper had put an extra couple of sweets in our bags today free of charge as a little good luck token for the show – nice little touch we thought and much appreciated. Mid refresher I spot Dunce and his merry men walking towards us – I nudge Gary trying to be discreet but he is so engrossed in his bag of tangfastics that I don't think he would of noticed a tornado!

"Looking forward to see your show today – should be good with all those props you got in that box" said Dunce with a smirk on his face.

How did he know we had a prop box or what we had in it? Gary said he's just trying

to freak us out before we go on – and I'm afraid it was working – well on me anyway. Gary thought that Dunce and his merry men had probably just seen us walking to school with the box this morning but I couldn't help but be suspicious of a suspected sabotage. Dunce wouldn't mention it for no reason – I mean they can't get their hands on it anyway because it's with the stage team, and that's headed by Mr. Hearne 'Bunsen

Burn' the biology teacher and he is freakishly tall with a large head of hair and a very deep voice, which put together makes for a rather scary looking character so I wouldn't imagine Dunce would get past him in a hurry – I hope.

Chapter 9

The Talent Show

The stage was set for act one, the hall was full of bums in seats with a row of parents lined along the back to show support and gloat at times. Both my mum and Gary's were stood right in front of the exit. I tried not to read too much into this and hoped it wasn't so she could make a quick getaway should I embarrass the family, but Gary said it's because his mum will be bored waiting for us to come on and won't last that long without going outside for a fag; I hate the smell of Gary's mum – I mean she's really cool and a nice person but her breath stinks and I have to hold my breath when she comes near me so I don't take any of it in! She literally can't go anywhere without her fags. Mum said it's called an addiction and it can kill you and it's really expensive! I just don't get it – bad breath, expensive and kills you – why would you bother!

Anyway after a (slightly) boring speech from our headmistress Mrs. Toft with her bright red lipstick and hair like a lion, the show was underway.

Helen Davies was up first singing 'her version' of 'I will always love you' by Whitney Houston, and although there was nothing different about 'her version' other than the fact that she's called Helen and not Whitney, she did a pretty good job and opened the show well with a round of applause and a thumbs up from the three teachers that had been allocated the job of judges for the day. I'm guessing that it's a name in a hat job for the picking process between the teachers, because every year they just try and be nice and encouraging – not like your typical judges you see on TV, all the drama is saved for the stage at our school.

The show continued to run smooth with only a few bum notes and forgotten choreography here and there, but all covered up pretty well in my opinion. Our time slot was drawing near and I started to get those butterflies in my stomach again. You can't really cover up a magic trick that goes wrong – the circumstances that come with a wrong move in my profession can be career threatening – this was some heavy weight pressure on my shoulders; but when I put my cloak and hat on I start to feel more ready and focused on my job – funny how a uniform can do that, give you confidence like an alter ego type thing. Gary was just enjoying watching the other acts, and at the end telling me whether we are better than them or if they are competition for the first prize.

I really envy the way Gary doesn't seem to

feel pressure or get nervous, and if he were then you would never know to look at him – a master of disguise that boy! I think he is genuinely just excited about doing the show. I guess the mixture of our two characters is why it works though – be no good if we were both too laid back – I'd forget which cup the ball was under!

Act fourteen was called to the side of the stage as the host of the show Mr. Owen introduced them, which meant we were up next! I was stood quietly gathering my thoughts and running through the act in my head, when I got a tap on the shoulder, I looked around and Dunce was stood in front of me.

"Good luck magic geeks – you're going to need it without all your props! Bit silly leaving that box lying around wasn't it – someone might take something out of it –

spoil your act and all that – be a shame to see you both look stupid in front of everyone!" Dunce said with the biggest grin on his face and his two idiot friends just stood either side of him going 'yeah, yeah'

As he walked off I turned to Gary, "I told you he was up to something didn't I. That's it the act is ruined what's the point in going on just to fall flat on our faces."

"We will be fine it's not that bad", said Gary "Ok so he's taken a few cups but we still have hanky up a sleeve and the card trick to do."

This was true, but it also meant that our act would run short of the allocated time allowed to each performer – I had an idea but Gary was just going to have to trust me – I whispered what I was thinking of and Gary just smiled, and said, *"Let's do it"*.

Mr. Owen introduced us as "Magicki" to

the stage and we took the ten steps forward from the side to centre stage with a round of applause. The hall was packed it looked so much busier head on – Gary turned on the music he had made for the show on the CD player at the back – I hadn't checked this before hand and wasn't sure if I was going to be pulling hankies out to Will.I.Am or Rod Stewart! Thankfully it was just instrumental music from Gary's computer at home – quite dramatic sounding actually – I was impressed.

We started with hanky up a sleeve – Gary was brilliant, pretending to pull at it with all his might because it was stuck – the crowd loved it – especially when he stopped half way – lent on the side of the stage and pretended to catch his breath!

Then on to the card trick, Gary chose a person in the crowd and I asked them to pick a card and memorize it. It was a girl from the year above us – I didn't know her but recognized her from around school, she was a pretty girl so I didn't want to mess this up – nice one Gary I thought – you had to pick the fittest bird in here – NO PRESSURE!

The card she picked was placed back in the pack and re-shuffled; I flicked through a few cards giving the illusion that I couldn't find the one she had chosen, I shrugged my shoulders, took my pointed hat off, sat on the edge of the stage and scratched my head – the audience laughed – then I jumped up and asked her to stand up and check her blazer pocket, and low and behold there it was her card the Jack of Hearts! BOOM! IN YOUR FACE! I looked at Gary and could tell exactly what he was thinking – this magic thing has a way with the ladies – we could be onto something here! HA!

The audience clapped and cheered for us, but as I turned my back to walk towards the table I spotted Dunce, Chunk and Death Breath Seth laughing from the side of the stage. They knew what was coming and were excited to watch us fail – I looked directly at him with my back still to the waiting audience and he shouted out so all could hear,

"Is that all – thought you had one more trick for us!"

I looked back around and saw my mum looking very confused and miming "shuffle cup" at me like I had a temporary loss of memory, but without further ado and not another look at Dunce I said,

"Well thank you for pointing that out from the side of the stage, and yes we were supposed to have another trick for you, but unfortunately that trick was sabotaged so

77

I'm afraid we have no other choice but to give you a better trick! (The crowd cheered – mum looked scared – Gary's mum was having a fag). For our next trick I am going to lift my brilliant assistant Gary two feet from the ground using no ropes or illusions – but bear with us because this is the first time I've done it with a person – only ever practiced on the neighbour's cat!" The audience laughed. I was serious though – poor Gary!

I asked that the lights be dimmed and a spot light be placed on Gary only; I needed to remain in the background, so I could focus the energy through me and into Gary if this was going to work. The music was stopped and silence lay over the hall like a blanket. I shut my eyes and took a deep breath. Gary was stood still, arms at his side looking directly at the audience. Then without further ado he began to rise up in mid air. I pulled both my arms out in front of me and turned my palms up to the ceiling and slowly raised them up in time with Gary – who for the first time since I have known him was lost for words and utterly gob smacked that this was working! Gary's mouth was wide open catching flies – shut it I kept thinking we're supposed to be professionals – he looked more shocked than anyone that it was working and he's part of the act! The audience gaspcd, and I slowly lowered Gary back down to the floor to a standing ovation and the loudest applause and cheering you have ever heard!

As soon as Gary's feet hit the floor he ran and high fived me saying *"Told you we would be alright – knew you had it in you!"*

"You weren't so bad yourself mate" I said, "A bit heavy though – next time no sweets before the show – you'll put my back out!"

We laughed – took a bow, and left the stage to a continuous wave of applause. We didn't hang around this time and bow more than once – leave them wanting more I thought.

As we walked off Dunce, Martin and Seth were still stood there – Seth and Martin with their mouths wide open looking at us in disbelief at what they had witnessed – Gary took this opportunity to put that polo mint into Seth's mouth. A job he had that he had waited so long to do – Gary said that it sizzled when it hit his tongue but hopefully it will work – maybe he should of put the packet in!

Damien grabbed my arm as we walked off and whispered in my ear "You're a fake and I'm going to reveal you to everyone, I've got my eye on you Ricki, this isn't the last you'll hear from me."

Now I could of got in a row and started defending myself and Gary for what we had just done, but you know what, I'm going to take my mum's advice and nod, smile and walk away from this one, because like she says people never like what they don't understand; and I let my work do all the talking today and Dunce trying to work out how I did that last trick to reveal me to all – well that's going to take him a long time so I guess I'm safe for the next year at least!

Chapter 10

The aftermath

Of course we won the talent show which was purely down to the last trick but still felt amazing and everyone at school was looking at Gary and I a little differently now – an air of magic around us you could say!

I'm not going to lie to you life at school was pretty different for us since the show – even some of the teachers were sickly sweet to us – which was cringe. I'm not really interested in all that though – I was quite happy with my life the way it was before.

Ali the shopkeeper was thrilled for us – he had heard about the last trick from other kids that go in his store, and we did make it into the local paper that Ali obviously sells in his shop. He had cut the article and picture out and put it in his window with a big sign saying "The magician shops here!" HA FUNNY! He's a cheeky beggar that Ali, trying to increase custom off the back of our

Bandel Evening News

Magicki Aim for the Stars

Giant Sweets Found

success – give him his due though – it worked, as other kids we're asking what sweets Gary and I ate and his sales had doubled – haven't seen my share of the profit though! Funny that! When I told him all about the show he just patted me on the back and said "Good job bruv" and gave us a bag of sweets on the house – blinding I thought, now we're talking – this I could get used too!

It's strange how people want to be your

friend when they think you're cool; obviously we still get the odd person who is a non believer, and Dunce just death stares me whenever he gets the chance but hasn't spoken a word to me since the talent show. Chunk and Seth on the other hand have tried to be nice on a few occasions, Gary said he thinks Chunk just wants to be mates with me so I can use magic to make his portion of chips bigger! He's probably got a point with that. I know who my real friend is though and I'm happy staying like that – the more friends you have the more birthday parties you have to go to; which isn't a bad thing because of the cake but now they know I can do magic tricks – they'll be working me like a donkey on Blackpool beach!

On the other hand Gary loved the attention and was nagging me to audition for the bigger talent shows on the TV – he was slowly turning from WA to agent but I just let him waffle on so he's happy and quietly do what I want anyway! It's only because some of the girls in our school had started to talk to Gary – something he definitely wasn't used too!

One girl in particular, Veronica is her name, had taken a real shine to Gary. Don't think if he was honest she's his dream bird – I'm not saying she's fallen out of the ugly tree or anything just maybe had a slap from a few branches on the way down, but she compliments him on his peak-less cap, and offers him some of her choc chip cookies almost every lunch time, so the girl's got her uses! The way to Gary's heart is definitely through his stomach but I'm keeping that quiet, as I'm not sure I want Veronica around all the time. It's nice to see Gary enjoying it all though, and as long as he realizes we still have a lot of work to do then we'll be fine – staying focused isn't always his strong point!

Mum was so pleased for us, and kept talking about how brilliant the last trick was whenever Nan was around just to annoy her. I was chuffed mum had come to the show because I wanted her to see that I'm actually pretty good at this, and although she can't ever know that I'm a Warlock, I still want her to be part of my shows; she has questioned me on a few occasions when we have been on our own, asking me how it worked and what not but I won't speak a word I just say it's magic!

"Well you're pretty good at it Ricki I must say, so if you want to make a career out of it I will support you all the way – and if you want any help preparing the tricks then I will help, you only have to ask." Mum said.

Crafty little line at the end there trying to get me to spill on my tricks, but I just do what I always do to her and tap the end of my nose, but this time I decided to repeat the Latin Magic Circle Motto that I have on my door at Warlock HQ to her,

"Indocilis Privata Loqui mum that's all I'm saying!"

"Well gracias senor Ricki, I can speak a little Spanish too you know" she says

"Ok mum, you got me there." NOT! LOL!

I'm happy that Gary pushed me to enter the talent show all them months ago. Looking back on the journey I think it's all been a good thing; show casing my talent to everyone even if it was only at school, has made me believe in myself a lot more, and concreted the fact that this is really what I was born to do. Although I still have a lot to learn, and a long journey ahead of me until I am a fully-fledged Warlock. I'm excited to take that trip and I am sure it will have ups and downs, but between my family and my best friend Gary I know we will get there. Who knows what the future will bring. Will Gary's Nan lose her leg? Will Dunce work out who I really am? Will Gary finally get a peak on his cap? I guess you'll just have to wait and see!

Until then, be good to yourself! ☺

Printed in Great Britain
by Amazon.co.uk, Ltd.,
Marston Gate.